Dragons Are Back!

The Best of Nick Toczek's Dragon Poems

Caboodle Books Ltd
Riversdale, 8 Rivock Avenue,
Steeton, BD20 6SA, UK.

This book presents the best of Nick Toczek's dragon poems. Almost all are drawn from several highly successful collections which were originally published by Macmillan. In all, he's had more than forty books published. His most recent, a political work for adult readers, was published by Routledge in the spring of 2016.

Nick's three previous poetry collections for Caboodle are all still in print. They are *Me and My Poems*, *Cat'n'Bats'n'Slugs'n'Bugs* and – particularly suitable for younger readers or those whose first language isn't English – *Number, Number, Cut a Cucumber*.

He's also a columnist, reviewer and features-writer for the UK music journal, *R2*. And, for the past twenty-five years, he's presented his own weekly show, *InTOCZEKated*, on BCB Radio, a community FM station based in his home town of Bradford in Yorkshire.

To find out more about him, check out his Wikipedia page: http://en.wikipedia.org/wiki/Nick_Toczek.

To find out more about his work in schools and his availability visit:
http://www.authorsabroad.com/authors/profile/nick-toczek.

For information on his political writings go to: http://www.routledge.com/products/9781138853508.

And to hear his recent radio shows go to http://www.bcbradio.co.uk and click 'listen again'. His show is called InTOCZEKated.

Contents

The Dragon who ate our School

The day the dragon came to call,
She ate the gate, the playground wall
And, slate by slate, the roof and all,
The staffroom, gym and entrance hall,
And every classroom, big or small.

So...
She's undeniably great,
She's absolutely cool,
The dragon who ate
The dragon who ate
The dragon who ate our school.

Pupils panicked. Teachers ran.
She flew at them with wide wingspan.
She slew a few and then began
To chew through the lollipop man,
Two parked cars and a transit van.

Wow... !
She's undeniably great,
She's absolutely cool,
The dragon who ate
The dragon who ate
The dragon who ate our school.

She bit off the head of the head.
She said she was sad he was dead.
He bled and he bled and he bled.
And, as she fed, her chin went red.
And then she swallowed the cycle shed.

Oh...
She's undeniably great,
She's absolutely cool,
The dragon who ate
The dragon who ate
The dragon who ate our school.

It's thanks to her that we've been freed.
We needn't write. We needn't read.
Me and my mates are all agreed,
We're very pleased with her indeed.
So clear the way. Let her proceed.

Cos...
She's undeniably great,
She's absolutely cool,
The dragon who ate
The dragon who ate
The dragon who ate our school.

There was some stuff she couldn't eat.
A monster forced to face defeat,
She spat it out along the street –
The dinner ladies' veg and meat
And that pink stuff they serve for sweet.

But...
She's undeniably great,
She's absolutely cool,
The dragon who ate
The dragon who ate
The dragon who ate our school.

Dragon on a Bus

Now, you know I'm not a wuss.
I don't like to make a fuss
But there's just a little matter that I think we should
        discuss...
There's a dragon on the bus!
There's a dragon on the bus!
There's a dragon on the bus and it's looking at us!

Let me speak to an inspector
Or the company director
Cos I don't quite recollect a
Sign to say we should expect a
Scaly people-vivisector on this bus.

Now, I never swear and cuss
But it's flipping obvious
That we've got a situation here that could be hazardous.
There's a dragon on the bus!
There's a dragon on the bus!
There's a dragon on the bus and it's coming after us!

I think we should call a meeting
Cos its fiery breath is heating
All our clothing and our seating.
I don't like the way it's treating
All the people that it's eating on this bus.

It's chewing us and burning us
And this is what's concerning us.
It could become a problem by the time we reach the
        terminus.
There's a dragon on the bus!
There's a dragon on the bus!
There's a dragon on the bus and it's eating
        and it's eating
                and it's eating all of us!

Dragons are Back

Alas, alack
The dragons are back
And any time now
They're bound to attack.
The sky will turn
From blue to black
With lightning-flash
And thunder-crack.

The dragons are back
The dragons are back
The dragons, the dragons
The dragons are back.

They snap their jaws
Snickerty-snack,
Flash their claws
Flickerty-flack,
Twitch their tails
Thwickerty-thwack,
Clank their scales
Clickerty-clack.

The dragons are back
The dragons are back
The dragons, the dragons
The dragons are back.

The mill goes still.
The wind is slack.
The cows won't milk.
The ducks don't quack.
We try to talk
But just lose track:
Go mumble jumble
Yakkity-yak.

The dragons are back
The dragons are back
The dragons, the dragons
The dragons are back.

We dare not stay.
We quickly pack.
But every road's
A cul-de-sac.
The priest has had
A heart attack.
The king's become
A maniac.

The dragons are back
The dragons are back
The dragons, the dragons
The dragons are back.

The Dragon in the Cellar

There's a dragon!
There's a dragon!
There's a dragon in the cellar!
Yeah, we've got a cellar-dweller.
There's a dragon in the cellar.

He's a cleanliness fanatic,
Takes his trousers and his jacket
To the dragon from the attic
Who puts powder by the packet
In a pre-set automatic
With a rattle and a racket
That's disturbing and dramatic.

There's a dragon!
There's a dragon!
There's a dragon in the cellar!
With a flame that's red 'n' yeller,
There's a dragon in the cellar...

... and a dragon on the roof
Who's only partly waterproof,
So she's borrowed an umbrella
From the dragon in the cellar.

There's a dragon!
There's a dragon!
There's a dragon in the cellar!
If you smell a panatela
It's the dragon in the cellar.

And the dragon from the study's
Helping out his cellar buddy
Getting wet and soap-suddy,
With the dragon from the loo
There to give a hand too,
While the dragon from the porch
Supervises with a torch,
Though the dragon from the landing
Through a slight misunderstanding
Is busy paint-stripping and sanding.

There's a dragon!
There's a dragon!
There's a dragon in the cellar!
Find my dad and tell the feller
There's a dragon in the cellar...

... where the dragon from my room
Goes zoom, zoom, zoom
In a cloud of polish and spray perfume
Cos he's the dragon whom
They pay to brighten up the gloom
With a mop and a duster and a broom,
broom, broom.

There's a dragon!
There's a dragon!
There's a dragon in the cellar!
Gonna get my mum and tell her
There's a dragon in the cellar.

Raggin' the Dragon

We come right up to the mouth of the cave.
We shout for him as if we're brave.
And he hates the way that we behave.
We make him rant. We make him rave.

We're raggin' the dragon.
We're raggin' the dragon.
We're giving the dragon some agony.

Raggin' the dragon is second-to-none.
It's all a game we learn for fun.
We call a name. We turn and run.
We shout:

"Old slug!
Scabby lug!
Cave Bug!
Ugly thug!

Bag on your head.
Bag on your head.
Face like a dragon," we said.

Raggin' the dragon is second-to-none.
It's all a game we learn for fun.
We call a name. We turn and run.
We shout:

"Worm tail!
Beached whale!

Hook-nail!
Smelly snail!"

Slaggin' you off.
Slaggin' you off.
"Call yourself a dragon?" we scoff.

Raggin' the dragon is second-to-none.
It's all a game we learn for fun.
We call a name. We turn and run.
We shout:

"Stink pot!
Body rot!
Hot snot!
Grumpy grot!

Smack in the snout!
Smack in the snout!
Raggedy dragon!" is what we shout.

Raggin' the dragon is second-to-none.
It's all a game we learn for fun.
We call a name. We turn and run.
We shout:

"Green yob!
Slimy slob!
Big blob!
Toothy gob!

Gag on your tongue!
Gag on your tongue!
Voice like a dragon!" we sung.

Raggin' the dragon is second-to-none.
It's all a game we learn for fun.
We call a name. We turn and run.

We're raggin' the dragon.
We're raggin' the dragon.
We're giving the dragon some agony.

They're out There

The ghosts of old dragons
Drift over this town,
Their wings grown as thin
As a princess's gown,
Their scaly skin leaf-like
And wintery-brown.

The ghosts of old dragons
Are flitting round town.
Their names are lost treasures,
Each glittering noun
Thrown deep in time's ocean
Where memories drown.

The ghosts of old dragons
Keep haunting this town,
Though long-gone like gas-lamp,
Top-hat and half-crown;
Their presence as false
As the face of a clown.

The ghosts of old dragons
Go growling through town,
As upright as tombstones
Engraved with a frown;
With gravel-path voices
Which wind travels down.

Ten Green Dragons

In the cave lived dragons ten.
One fell fighting four horsemen.

In the cave lived dragons nine.
One went down the deep dark mine.

In the cave lived dragons eight.
Two forgot to hibernate.

In the cave lived dragons six.
One dropped dead from politics.

In the cave lived dragons five.
One took a dive in overdrive.

In the cave lived dragons four.
One got struck by a meteor.

In the cave lived dragons three.
One ran off with a chimpanzee.

In the cave lived dragons two.
One went onto the king's menu.

In the cave lived dragon one.
Laid ten eggs and then was gone.

Being a Dragon

Being a dragon is cool as ice.
Being a dragon is nice, nice, nice.
Whatever it costs, it's worth the price
Cos being a dragon is nice.

When you're a dragon it's fine to fly.
Bag the best wings money can buy.
Drop 'em in a vat of sky-green dye
Then hang them, bat-like, out to dry.
Shoofly pie. Shoofly pie.
When you're a dragon it's fine to fly.

Being a dragon is cool as ice.
Being a dragon is nice, nice, nice.
Whatever it costs, it's worth the price
Cos being a dragon is nice.

When you're a dragon, you love your claws.
Use hardware stores when stealing yours.
The stainless ones are best for wars,
Settling scores and breaking laws.
Patio doors. Patio doors.
When you're a dragon, you love your claws.

Being a dragon is cool as ice.
Being a dragon is nice, nice, nice.
Whatever it costs, it's worth the price
Cos being a dragon is nice.

When you're a dragon, you gargle fire.
Never buy flames, it's better to hire.
Ignite the tobacco in an old man's briar
And later light his funeral pyre.
Tractor tyre. Tractor tyre.
When you're a dragon, you play with fire.

Being a dragon is cool as ice.
Being a dragon is nice, nice, nice.
Whatever it costs, it's worth the price
Cos being a dragon is nice.

The Week of the Dragon

Monday's dragon was just an egg
Not unlike a chicken's. Were they pulling my leg?

Tuesday's dragon hatched one inch high
With crumpled wings which wouldn't fly
And a roar little more than a squeaky cry.

Wednesday's dragon was the size of a cat.
Passers-by paused at the sight of that.
When a woman bent down to give it a pat
It hissed and spat at her and lit her hat.

Thursday's dragon grew bigger than a goat
With a shiny scaly bright green coat.
It grew too fast. For an antidote
We saw the vet, but all she wrote was a useless note
Prescribing stuff to cool its throat.

Friday's dragon filled our whole street,
Lamp-posts flattening beneath its feet,
Porches scorched by nostril heat.
It'd eaten all of the butcher's meat
And a child who'd tried to offer it a sweet
And next-door's dog as an after-dinner treat.

Saturday's dragon, having learned to fly,
Hovered overhead and blotted out the sky.
Its beating wings! Its terrifying cry!
We were all convinced we were going to die,

But luckily for us, my family and I,
None of this happened. Let me tell you why...
It WAS a chicken's egg. They'd told me a lie!

So Sunday's dragon wasn't there at all,
'til a strange man selling eggs came to call...

The Dragon's Curse

Enter darkness. Leave the light.
Here be nightmare. Here be fright.
Here be dragon, flame and flight.
Here be spitfire. Here be grief.
So curse the bones of unbelief.
Curse the creeping treasure-thief.
Curse much worse the dragon-slayer.
Curse his purse and curse his payer.
Curse these words. Preserve their sayer.
Earth and water, fire and air.
Prepare to meet a creature rare.
Enter now, if you dare.
Enter now... the dragon's lair!

Dragon at the Swimming Pool

He jumps in with a great big splash.
The waves make several windows smash.
His flame goes out. He coughs grey ash
That lends his lip a thick moustache.

Wings and the water-surface crash
Like cymbals giant drummers bash
Or shields when two great armies clash
Or thunder after lightning's flash.

The water's cold. His teeth all gnash.
He shakes his tail, makes it whiplash
Which churns the pool like making mash
And scales break free like scattered cash.

When all four claws begin to thrash
The lifeguard gains a nasty gash,
So swimmers flee, spectators dash.
Panic rules. It's a total hash.

That clumsy beast lacks all panache.
To let him swim was worse than rash.
There should be rules. It's so slapdash.
No dragon ban? That's balderdash!

Finding a Dragon's Lair

The way to find a dragon's lair
Is down the road that goes nowhere,
Over the bridge called Curse-And-Swear
On the river of Deep Despair.

Take the track to Give-You-A-Scare
Across the marsh of Say-A-Prayer,
Over the peak of Past Repair
And down the cliff of Do Beware.

Through the valley of If-You-Dare
You'll find the town of Don't-Go-There
Where folk won't speak but stand and stare
And nobody will be Lord Mayor.

Beyond lies land that's parched and bare,
A dried up lake named None-To-Spare,
A rock that's known as Life's Unfair
And hills they call No-Longer-Care.

It's hard to breathe the dreadful air
And in the sun's relentless glare
The heat becomes too much to bear.
You'll not be going anywhere.

You're weak and dazed but just aware
Of something moving over there
Approaching to inspect its snare...
And then you smell the dragon's lair.

Dragons Everywhere

Mrs Meacher, our gym teacher,
Looks at you like she might eatcha.
Anger alters every feature.
She becomes another creature –
Winged avenger, screamer, screecher.
Burning breath, much more than warm,
She blisters pupils in her form.
If she's a human, I'm a unicorn.

Then there's Gordon, traffic warden,
Ordinary 'n' dull with boredom,
Till he roared 'n' ripped 'n' clawed 'n'
Ran amok, all lightning-jawed 'n'
Flaming tongued 'n' toothed 'n' clawed 'n'
Frightening as a thunderstorm.
But underneath his uniform
If there's a human, I'm a unicorn.

Mrs Ritter, babysitter,
TV watcher, silent knitter.
I know why her clothes don't fit her.
She's another fire-spitter,
Beastly, battle-scarred and bitter.
Her bat-like wings have both been shorn,
But I know that she's dragon-spawn.
If she's a human, I'm a unicorn.

Mouse-man Mervyn, dressed in rat skin,
Brings his traps in, catches vermin,
Scratches his reptilian chin
With fingernails grown long and thin,
His bloodshot eyes, his evil grin.
A twisted figure, worn and torn,
Who can't recall where he was born.
If he's a human, I'm a unicorn.

Miss McPeake, our glum shopkeeper,
Avaricious treasure-heaper,
Piles 'em high and sells 'em cheaper.
People-server and floor-sweeper,
Deep down, though, she'd be Grim Reaper.
Customers all sense her scorn.
One day they'll meet her with claws drawn.
If she's a human, I'm a unicorn.

The family that lives next door
Seem quite alright, but nightly roar
And smoke stains ruin their décor.
And each of them's a carnivore –
I've seen them eating meat that's raw.
A mountain cave on the Matterhorn
Is where each first saw the light of dawn.
If they're all human, I'm a unicorn.

And, as for me, I'm feeling strange,
All aches and pains and bad migraines.
Soon parts of me will start to change,
My limbs and body rearrange,
And I'll become quite dangerous,
Grow rows of teeth like rose-bush thorns
And skin as tough as rhino horn,
And be a dragon, not a unicorn.

Blubberbelly Wobblewalk Stumblebum Smith

When I was young, I made friends with
Blubberbelly Wobblewalk Stumblebum Smith,
A proper live dragon, not just a myth.

Lonely and large as a monolith,
Blubberbelly Wobblewalk Stumblebum Smith
Had no parents, kin or kith.

One day I was cruel. He left forthwith,
Blubberbelly Wobblewalk Stumblebum Smith,
For a secret place he called his frith.

I often wish I'd made up with
Blubberbelly Wobblewalk Stumblebum Smith
Who never returned after our daft tiff.

Was he real or merely a myth?
Blubberbelly Wobblewalk Stumblebum Smith,
The dragon I used to be friends with.

The Child who pretended to be a Dragon

My mum and dad got angry
And they told me not to lie
When I said that I'd grown wings
And was learning how to fly.

They said I should be sensible
And stop making a fuss
After I'd announced that I was green
And longer than a bus.

And they turned around and told me
I was not to tell tall tales
When they heard that I'd been claiming
That my skin was growing scales.

Then both of them got cross with me
And each called me a liar
Just because I mentioned
I'd been breathing smoke and fire.

But they finally got flaming mad,
They really hit the roof
When I rushed at them with sharpened claws
And all my teeth, as proof.

My mum let out a piercing scream.
My dad began to rave.
So I ate them both. They tasted nice.
Then I flew off to live in a cave.

Dragon

Dragon has spikes all down her back,
Has claws in her paws that she draws to attack.
She's scaly, savage and sickly green,
Merciless, mindless, cruel and mean.

Dragon is heartless, has no soul.
Her red eyes glow like burning coal.
Her body is built with bulletproof scales.
She can pound you to pulp with one swish of her tail.

Dragon has a furnace fitted in each lung,
A flickering, forked and fireproof tongue,
Crocodile jaws from which she pours
Great searing flames and frightful roars.

Dragon's cave is a reeking trench
With a dank, sulphurous, smoky stench
Made fouler by the crevices and cracks
Where rotting limbs are stored for snacks.

Dragon loves her cavernous lair,
Keeps her heaps of treasure there,
Hardly sleeps for fear of thieves,
Needs to be ravenous before she leaves.

When dragon spreads her dreadful wings
Death will be what her hunger brings.
Breathlessly she pursues warm flesh.
She wants it human, young and fresh.

Dragon spies people far beneath.
She flies down, claws first, followed by teeth.
She grips and grinds. She chomps and chews,
Spits belt-buckles, buttons and shoes.

Dragon finally finishes feeding,
Splattered red from all their bleeding,
Flies home slowly with a bloated gut,
Reaches the entrance to her darkness... but...

Dragon, sensing men and horses,
Sniffs the air... sniffs, then pauses...
A stink, she thinks, not normally there...
A man somewhere inside her lair!

When a dragon stares into her breath,
Her life up to the point of death
Appears before her in the smoke –
The future pulling back its cloak.

Dragon breathes... The picture clears
But lacks its usual months and years.
Instead, she sees reflected back
Mere moments, then a sea of black.

Dragon-slayer draws his bow,
Aims, and lets the arrow go.
It flies to where the scaly coat
Is weakest, at the creature's throat.

Dragon feels the fateful flood,
The sea of black, the flow of blood,
And, far below, the undertow
Of pain, from bolt and piercing blow.

Dragon falls and twists about.
Her fire chokes and flickers out.
She coughs a cloud of smoke. She sighs,
Then lies quite still, with staring eyes.

The slayer slices off her head
To make quite certain that she's dead.
These killings bring him little pleasure.
He never dares to touch their treasure.

He doesn't like the job as such.
It doesn't earn him very much.
And, with each dragon, goes a curse,
So, death by death, his life grows worse.

"Why does he do it?", you may ask.
Well, someone has to do the task.

He breaks her eggs. He blocks her cave.
He buries her body in a shallow grave,
Shoves the head in a blood-stained sack
And leads his horse back down the track.

Scaly Skin

I have a toothsome evil grin
And blood around my lips and chin
That is of human origin.
It trickles down my scaly skin.

I've eyes as sharp as any pin.
They're hard and red and dark as sin.
I'm roguish as a Rasputin:
A devil in a scaly skin.

My roar's a deep explosive din
That mixes nitroglycerin
With flaming tongues of paraffin
So hot they scorch my scaly skin.

My cries that rise so high and thin –
Like madness on a violin
Or bagpipes with no discipline –
Send shivers down my scaly skin.

But I've a toothsome evil grin
And blood around my lips and chin
That is of human origin.
It trickles down my scaly skin.

Slow Service at the Tortoise Garage

In the German township of Kassel
Just two blocks down from The Dragon Hotel
On the forecourt of the tortoise Shell
Petrol station, Mademoiselle
The Countess Lady Isabel,
Dragoness de Neufchatel,
Has been waiting quite a lengthy spell
In her pink Volkswagen Caravelle.

She sips a glass of muscatel,
Having told her toad chauffeur, Marcel,
That she thought he ought to jolly well
Get out and ring that service bell
And tell the slowcoach personnel
To hurry up and – what-the-hell –
Raise his voice and really yell
The French word "Vite!", the German "Schnell!"

This, she's sure, should now propel
These tortoises to serve and sell
Some petrol for her Caravelle,
A faith which time will soon dispel
For tortoises, unlike gazelle,
So gradually shift, you can hardly tell.
More slothful than sloths, they're without parallel,
Their slowness the one thing at which they excel.

If you're in a hurry, avoid Kassel,
The city in which the tortoises dwell.
Why, it'll be hours before Mademoiselle
The Countess Lady Isabel,
Dragoness de Neufchatel,
And her put-upon chauffeur, poor Marcel,
Can bid that flat forecourt farewell
And drive off past The Dragon Hotel.

Maybe You're a Dragon

If your voice is grumpy
If your claws are clumpy
If your back is bumpy
Maybe you're a dragon.

If your cheeks are chumpy
If your tail is thumpy
If your head is humpy
Maybe you're a dragon.

If your body's dumpy
If your waddle's rumpy
If your breath is trumpy
Maybe you're a dragon.

If your legs are stumpy
If your shape is frumpy
If your tummy's plumpy
Maybe you're a dragon.

If your skin is mumpy
If your jaws are jumpy
If your face is lumpy
Maybe you're a dragon.

Roaring like Dragons

On the count of four, I want you all to roar.
One... two... three... four...

No! Not the squawk of a fowl
Or the hoot of an owl
Or the half-choked note of a bleating goat
Or the moody moo that a cow'll do.
That was very, very poor.
I fare better when I snore.
What I want is a proper roar.
One... two... three... four...

No, no, no! Not a toothsome scowl
Or a long loud vowel
Or the screech of creatures
When a beast is on the prowl.
Call that your best? I'm far from sure.
It didn't thrill me to the core.
Now gimme a roar I can't ignore.
One... two... three... four...

Pathetic! Did I ask for a yell or a yelp or a yowl?
Did I call for a caterwaul, holler or howl
Or a burp or a belch
From a belly or a bowel?
Now rattle the windows and the door.
Shake the ceiling and the floor.
Show your jaw what your lungs are for.
One... two... three... four...

Hmm. That felt fierce and forcefully foul.
I'd call that a fabulously fearsome growl.
But did it rip your lips up?
No! Did it jellify your jowl?
No! Well, sorry to be a bit of a bore,
But I think you can guess what I've got in store,
That I'm going to ask you for even more.
So be louder than the crowd when the home team score.
Make a shockwave worse than the Third World War.
Do astounding sounds like dragons galore.
Roar and roar as never before.
Roar and roar till your throats are sore.
One... two... three... four...

Encore!

Encore!

Encore!

The American Dragon

Elephantine, with a burger belly,
He sits in New York, watching telly –
A graceless beast in a room that's smelly.

This figure far bigger than a Botticelli
Is fed fatty food from his local deli –
Fries and pizza and tagliatelle.

His weak wings flap like a pair of umbrelli,
For a flightless wobble by a bright green jelly
With more spare tyres than anyone requires...
Even the suppliers of Pirelli!

He's jealous of the elegance of Gene Kelly
And longs to be lithe like Liza Minnelli
Or to flaunt a physique like football's Pele.

But elephantine, with a burger belly,
He sits in New York, watching telly –
This graceless beast in a room that's smelly.

Finding a Dragon to Finish our Food

We're children. We're choosy.
We're fussy. We're picky,
Don't want food that's oozy
Or slimy or sticky,
Leave heaps and whole slices
From each of those courses
You serve up in spices
Or herbs or thick sauces.
Whatever you make us,
Just count yourself lucky
If we don't pull faces
Or moan that it's yucky.

Yet you say it's rude of us, leaving our food,
But who'll nosh our noodles or feed on our peas?
We need a fine dragon who'll dine on all these:
Our spam, spuds and spinach, our strong stinky cheese,
Large lumpy dumplings, great globs of cold custard,
Leeks, lentils, lettuces, mushrooms and mustard.

You'd best find a beast that you know licks its lips
At kippers, crab-sticks and asparagus tips,
Parsnips and turnips and marrows and swedes,
Haggises, cabbages, cress and such weeds.
With luck it'll suit the great big-bellied brute
To pig out on pork pies and purple beetroot.
Go bring us a beastie to sit up and beg
For the runniest bit of our breakfast boiled egg.

We're children. We're choosy.
We're fussy. We're picky,
Don't want food that's oozy
Or slimy or sticky,

Drag out a dragon that's certain to rid me
Of slithery liver, leathery kidney,
One who'll devour a whole cauliflower
And then be quite barmy for brawn or salami,
Mad about Marmite, mincemeat, minestrone,
Prunes, prawns and porridge and cold macaroni.
We need, now, a creature who'll go cock-a-hoop
For oysters and olives and old oxtail soup,
A beast keen on onions and dark aubergines,
Broccoli, rhubarb, black pudding, broad beans,
Cockles and mussels and salady greens,
Horseradish sauce and whole tins of sardines.

Whatever you make us,
Just count yourself lucky
If we don't pull faces
Or moan that it's yucky.

Please help us to find a fine beast of the kind
To polish off platefuls of thick bacon-rind,
Eat all our meatballs and our Yorkshire puddin',
Gobble our gherkins and grapefruit; a good 'un,
A huge hot-breath creature, one who won't worry
When given a gallon of vindaloo curry.
Yes, we've a fine feast for our full-bellied beast
Merrily munchin' a celery luncheon.
Why, I bet this dragon's great fireproof snout
Could even consume an entire Brussels sprout!

We're children. We're choosy.
We're fussy. We're picky,
Don't want food that's oozy
Or slimy or sticky,

But bring us a dragon that's willing to eat
Our vilest of veges, our fattiest meat,
Our foulest of fruits, our unsavoury sweet
And mealtimes would magically turn out a treat.

A Poem to Whisper

Shhh!

All the dragons are fast asleep,
Each curled up on a golden heap
Of treasure that these creatures keep.

Shhh!

All the dragons are fast asleep.
Their cave is dark. Their cave is deep –
A chimney-stack we've come to sweep.

Shhh!

All the dragons are fast asleep.
We crowd outside like silent sheep
And warily, by torchlight, peep.

Shhh!

All the dragons are fast asleep.
With weapons in our hands, we creep
Down corridors cut cold and steep.

Shhh!

All the dragons are fast asleep.
We reach their lair and start to reap,
And each one dies without a peep.

Shhh!

All the dragons are fast asleep
And rivulets of red blood seep
Through riches, proving life is cheap.

Shhh!

All the dragons are fast asleep
And, though my friends all whoop and leap,
For some strange reason, I could weep.

Shhh!

Acting as if We're Dragons

Let's imagine that we're dragons. See who's best.
Pretend you're fast asleep inside your nest...
Then stretch as you emerge from reptile rest...
Yawn... and growl from deep inside your chest...
Press your stomach... dream of something to digest...

Shake yourself... and breathe out thick, black smoke...
Cough a bit... because it makes you choke.
Then rub your eyes... and move like you just woke...

Slowly stare out from you mountain lair...
Snarl... and try to make your nostrils flare...
Now suck... to fill your fiery lungs with air...

Let's see you exercise your lethal claws...
Expose those rows of teeth between your jaws...
Then scratch your ancient scars from dragon wars...

Stand up slowly... huge, and hard as nails.
Flex those muscles underneath your scales...
Now set you sights on distant hills and vales...

And flap your arms as if they're heavy wings...
Listen to the way the high wind sings...
As you now fly... towards the lands of kings.

Lick your lips... and keep your cruel eyes peeled...
Though you need to feed, your wounds have hardly
    healed
From your fight with a knight with sword and shield.

Fly on...

You're dizzy and weak before you arrive.
This time, you wonder if you will survive.
It's dangerous to hunt in the human hive.

Fly on...

Your hunger hurts... it stabs your guts like five hundred
    knives.
See that food below you...? Go into a dive...
Rip apart everything down there alive!

The Myth of Creation

A dragon flew out of the sun
And from its flames whole worlds were spun
And from its names were words begun
With all we've thought and said and done
And wars were fought and lost and won
And tales were taught and lies were spun
That a dragon flew out of the sun.

What have we got in the house?

I think I know what we've got in the house.
When it moves, it makes more mess than a mouse.
So what do you think we've got in the house?

We found eggshell down
By the washing machine
And four claw-prints
In the margarine.

I think I know what we've got in the house.
When it moves, it makes more mess than a mouse
Or a rat or a roach or a louse.
So what do you think we've got in the house?

The sides of the bath
Are greenish-tinged
And the spare toothbrush
Has had its bristles singed.

I think I know what we've got in the house.
When it moves, it makes more mess than a mouse
Or a rat or a roach or a louse
Or a gerbil or an oyster or a grouse.
So what do you think we've got in the house?

We've never had a fire
But I often cough,
Then the smoke alarm
In the hall goes off.

I think I know what we've got in the house.
When it moves, it makes more mess than a mouse
Or a rat or a roach or a louse
Or a gerbil or an oyster or a grouse
Or a duck-billed platypus together with its spouse.
So what do you think we've got in the house?

There are long scratch-marks
Just like from claws
Around the handles
Of all the doors.

I think I know what we've got in the house.
Do you?

The Sound of Sleeping Dragons

Asleep on deep dark dungeon floors,
Our dragons dream, like dinosaurs,
Their wordless reveries of roars...

A punctuation of bold snores
That grumbles out of gaping jaws
And tumbles down cold corridors.

The sound of sleeping,
Sound of sleeping,
Sound of sleeping dragons.

It rumbles round their treasure-stores.
It crumbles roofs. It rattles doors.
It leaks outside like loud applause.

It echoes over lakes and moors.
It crests the peaks where eagle soars
To fade beyond the farthest shores.

The sound of sleeping,
Sound of sleeping,
Sound of sleeping dragons.

Life and Death

They felt few emotions.
Their blood was corrosive.
Their dreams were deep oceans.
Their breath was explosive.

Their land lay uncharted.
Their caves were like sewers.
Their sleep was hard-hearted.
Their claws were like skewers.

Their hunger was boundless,
Their lives melodrama.
Their flight was quite soundless.
Their scales were their armour.

Their tails were like rivers,
Their flames like bright fountains.
Their cries caused cold shivers.
Their wealth was worth mountains.

Their instinct was grasping.
Their airspace was birdless.
Their voices were rasping.
Their language was wordless.

Their eyes were like lazers.
Their minds were infernal.
Their teeth were like razors,
Their wisdom eternal,

Their fighting ferocious,
Their battleground blazing.
Their deaths were atrocious,
Though they were amazing.

Modern Dragons

Modern dragons act all flash,
Swish around with wads of cash,
Splash out rashly, dish the dosh,
Push for posh and pricy nosh.

They've more money than they've senses,
Have expensive residences,
High-class caves to suit the choosy –
Bidet, sauna and jacuzzi.
Wall-to-wall, these works of art
Are sumptuous, deluxe and smart.

Modern dragons of both sexes
Need fine jewellery, nice Rolexes,
Diamonds on their necks and wrists,
Gold rings clustered round their fists,
Pearl-encrusted treasure chests
Thrust in niches in their nests.

Modern dragons, draped in jewels,
Laze by heated swimming pools,
Sip Bacardis and Martinis,
Lounge around in Lambourghinis.
There's not much they can't afford
And all their claws are manicured.

Modern dragons own racehorses,
Drive to parties in green Porches
Or Ferraris or Rolls-Royces,
Talk in crisp and cultured voices,
Carve out consonant and vowel.
Modern dragons never growl.

With bodylines all redefined
Our dragons now are quite refined.
They've had their awkward wings removed.
They call it 'surgically improved'.
They've also been unspiked, untailed,
Their skins made paler and descaled,
Body-fat redistributed,
Teeth filed flat, false hair recruited.

Snake-skin booted, silken suited,
They socialise, their fire muted.

Modern dragons cruise and jet.
They never work. They never sweat.
Their world is one devoid of debt
Where everything they want, they get –
A world so small, there is no threat.
They never need to get upset.
The only things that make them fret
Are status, style and etiquette.

How Dragons hide from Us

Dragons Portuguese and Spanish,
Like the Cheshire Cat, can vanish.
Russian dragons, though they're large,
Are very skilled at camouflage.
And Chinese dragons, to escape,
Become old folk by changing shape.

Dragons Northern European,
Caribbean and Andean,
Hebridean and Fijian,
Galilean and Korean
Can shrink until they're minuscule
Then hide beneath a small toadstool.

Those from Corfu and Katmandu,
Mogadishu, Timbuktu,
Honolulu, Timaru,
And Machu Picchu in Peru,
Plus a few from Gazankulu
And one who's called Bartholemew
Can turn transparent, quite see-through.

While English dragons, being green,
Can hide in envy, quite unseen.
But their Welsh cousins, painted red,
Can't hide at all. So they're all dead.
Yet dragons from the USA
 Just scream at us and run away.

Dragon at a Party

Sidles in slowly and slyly and seedily
Wanders round wilily, wheedling wheezily
Grinning and greeting all gratingly greasily
Chummily, cheerily chattering cheesily

Leerily, beerily back-biting easily
Simpering simply salaciously sleazily
Pedalling scandal unpleasantly pleasedly
Eavesdropping evilly, eyes popping beadily

Hears his hosts' infant is in bed, diseasedly
Creeps upstairs sneakily, creakily, weaselly
Finds where the poor mite is quarantined queasily
Quiets their darling, his teeth closing tweezerly

Blood, flesh and bone are all cleared away speedily
Lovingly licked up and guzzled down greedily.
Dragons don't mind their meat sickly or measily...

"Wonderful party!" he tells them all breezily
Slips through the door and leaves, easy-peasily.

The Death of a Scottish Dragon

A young

Dragon named Keith
With hundreds of teeth
Above and beneath

His tongue,

Lived north of Leith
Till killed on the heath
Near cold Cowdenbeath.

They flung

Earth onto Keith
Took a sword from its sheath
And on it a wreath

Was hung.

Evidence

Dragon in computer games.
Places bearing dragon names.
Dragon used as skin tattoo.
Ship to carry Viking crew.
Sleeping now, but when it wakes,
Starts up storms and makes earthquakes.

Dragon drawn on early maps.
Gardens where the dragon snaps.
Ponds patrolled by dragonflies.
Dragon donning human guise.
Serpent circling the globe.
Dragon on a Chinese robe.

Dragon flown as paper kite.
Effigy in tribal rite.
Dragon as a kids' cartoon.
Origin of word 'dragoon'.
Dragon that the hero slew.
Biggest thing that ever flew.

Dragon landing on your roof.
You still saying: "Bring me proof!"

Speaking Dragonese

And do you do just as you please?
And are you keen on killing sprees?
And do you speak in Dragonese?

Do you, as each of us agrees,
Enjoy these joyless jamborees,
Pursuing everyone who flees,
A heartless sword of Damocles
Descending on these refugees?
And do you speak in Dragonese?

And of the people whom you seize,
Do you chew through each of these
As though they were just chunks of cheese?
And are your legs like trunks of trees,
Your hide as hard as manganese?
And do you speak in Dragonese?

Are you immune to most disease,
An unkind kind of Hercules,
A piece of slime, a slice of sleaze,
Whose mind despises all it sees
Through eyes as cold as dungeon keys?
And do you speak in Dragonese?

Does weather warm a few degrees
Whenever you so much as sneeze?
And is your breath the devil's breeze,
A howling, haunted, heated wheeze,
A wind to blow till Hell shall freeze?
And do you dream in Dragonese?

The Beastly Dragon

The dragon, the dragon's a beastly beast,
Its face all crumpled up and creased.
It should be jailed and not released.
Instead, it's out there unpoliced.

The dragon, the dragon's a beastly beast,
A fire-breathing, winged artiste
That's dangerous, to say the least.
It thinks of people as a feast.

The dragon, the dragon's a beastly beast
That has no faith in church or priest,
And, though their numbers have decreased,
They're still out west and in the east.

The dragon, the dragon's a beastly beast
That feeds on food that's not deceased,
Till caked in blood and thoroughly greased,
Its temper worse, its size increased.

The dragon, the dragon's a beastly beast.
From life that's found in lumps of yeast
To rhino, whale and wildebeest,
The dragon, the dragon's the beast of beasts.

Dragon eating Fish-n-Chips

See dragon scoffing fish-n-chips.
He slashes with his claws and rips
The paper wrapping off in strips,
Reveals his meal and promptly dips
Right in with eager talon-tips,
Locates his target, grabs and grips
Scissor-like with snipperty-snips,
And lobs each load between his lips
Like building workers filling skips.

Hear dragon gobble fish-n-chips,
Not dainty like their ladyships.
He chomps and chews. He slurps and sips
While pausing just to lick the drips
Of vinegar from smoke-stained lips.
Then, past his tongue, each gobful flips
And down his throat it loudly slips
Where countless meals have made such trips
To fatten belly, broaden hips.

Watch dragon wolf down fish-n-chips.
Such is his greed, he often strips
Potato farms and fishing ships.
He's like some vast apocalypse
That steals our food, that nicks, that whips,
That no disaster can eclipse.
"Today, I ate your fish-n-chips.
Tomorrow, I shall dine..." he quips
"On people-meat!" and smacks his lips.

Troglodytic Owner-Occupier

Old flier with a bellyful of fire
That's hotter than a deep-fat fryer,
Your tongue is tougher than a tyre,
Thicker and harder and drier.
You've the appetite of a vampire.

Old flier with a bellyful of fire,
You're driven by desire to acquire.
You trickster, rogue and liar.
You've eyes like snakes', but slyer.

Old flier with a bellyful of fire,
Mister mayhem multiplier.
Your cry's a terrifier,
The sound of a suffering choir
Entangled in barbed wire.

Old flier with a bellyful of fire,
Soaring higher that church and spire,
You're lord and magnifier,
His dragonship esquire,
Whom we, in awe, admire.

What Reg Says

There *are* still some dragons,
Or so Reg alleges.
These nest inaccessibly
On mountain ledges,
Or in polar regions
Not accessed by sledges,
Or hidden in marshland
By tall reeds and sedges.

And sometimes you find them,
Or so Reg alleges,
In caves under oceans
At depths no-one dredges,
Or in crumbling castles
Behind walls and hedges
With 'KEEP OUT!' and 'PRIVATE!' signs
All round the edges.

And some live down our way,
Or so Reg alleges,
Their neighbours all made to
Sign secrecy pledges.
These creatures eat pizzas,
Potato fried wedges,
And chicken and burgers
And stuff cooked for vegies.

And sometimes small people...
Or so Reg alleges.

The Strength of Dragons

All them dragons, 'ard as nails,
Bend steel girders wi' their tails,
Green in England, red in Wales,
'omes in caves and dungeon jails.

All them dragons, built like bricks,
'atch from eggs as monstrous chicks,
Vandalising lunatics,
Eyes as cold as old oil slicks.

All them dragons, tough as boots,
Bullet-proof in scaly suits,
Are cruel, calculating brutes,
Vile and vicious in disputes.

All them dragons, rough as rocks,
Body parts like concrete blocks,
Each wi' gob o' teeth what locks
Tight as bank-vault or strong box.

All them dragons, 'ard as nails,
Reek o' smoke and old entrails,
'oarding gold and guarding grails,
Wingspan wide as galleon sails.

All them dragons, built like bricks,
Knock 'ole villages for six,
'eadbut castle walls for kicks,
Smash 'em like they're mere matchsticks.

All them dragons, tough as boots,
Meet up cos they're in cahoots,
Share nefarious pursuits,
Night-time flights down secret routes.

All them dragons, rough as rocks,
Anything but orthodox,
When they gang in flaming flocks,
Armoured knights are laughing-stocks.

What can a Dragon do for a Living?

What can a dragon do for a living?
What can a dragon do?

Not get a job in London Zoo.
Not sell as shirt or a skirt or a shoe.
Not be a porter in Waterloo.

So what can a dragon
What can a dragon
What can a dragon do?

The problem's got him in a proper stew.
He's more hopping mad than a kangaroo.

So what can a dragon
What can a dragon
What can a dragon do?

He could be a cigarette lighter
But he's far too big for your pocket.
He could be a plane – say a fighter –
But he's not got a gun or a rocket.

So what can a dragon
What can a dragon
What can a dragon do?

His breath is a fiery brew.
He could warm your house for you.
But the curtains'd certainly scorch
And the furniture blacken like coke.
He might work as a light or a torch
Though we'd choke in a cloak of his smoke.

So what can a dragon
What can a dragon
What can a dragon do
To stay off the dole queue?

He could join a security crew
To guard the valued possessions
Of those in positions of wealth…
But dragons have treasure obsessions.
He'd just want it all for himself.
He'd say "This stuff is divine. It's ever so fine.
I'm making it mine. You can't have it back!"
So the boss would have to give him the sack.
He'd shout "Get out! Get out! Get out!
The dragon's no good! Now see that he leaves!
How can we have guards who turn into thieves?"

So what can a dragon
What can a dragon
What can a dragon do?

When summer's well and truly through,
When rainclouds form and a storm is due,
He could be a useful feller,
Spread his wings, be a green umbrella…
But he's ever so heavy to hold;

Or maybe a newspaper seller,
But in the freezing cold
He'd turn from green to blue
Then probably get the flu
And go "Achoo! Achoo! Achoo!
This job's no good! I need something new."

So what can a dragon
What can a dragon
What can a dragon do?
What career can he pursue?

Well, I really wish I knew
But I simply haven't a clue.
What work have we got for the creature?
The problem is proving too tough.
He could have a job as teacher…
But I know he's not nasty enough!

So what can a dragon
What can a dragon
What can a dragon do?
I dunno. Do you?

I've seen a Dragon in Farmer James's Field

Says dad: There are no dragons now.
             You saw Farmer James's cow.

Says I: But, dad, I've never seen
             A cow of quite that shade of green.

Says mum: There are no dragons now.
             You saw Farmer James's sow.

Says I: Since when did any pig
             Possess a pair of wings that big?

Says gran: There are no dragons now.
             You saw Farmer James's plough.

Says I: If so, then what I saw
             Was a plough that had been taught to
             roar.

Says sis: There are no dragons now,
             But the farmer's cat has a loud miaow.

Says I: If we've no dragons now,
             Then please will someone tell me how
             The farmer's cat can breathe out flames
             And why it's eating Farmer James.

Truth and Lies about Dragons

When I look at you,
Can you tell by my eyes
Whether this is true
Or a pack of lies…?

Your Chinese dragon, chum, I'll cheerfully confirm,
Is a big, bright and blustery, breezy worm.
We had one at school, but it left last term,
Got a good job with a Birmingham firm.

We've bird-like dragons with feathers and beaks
That nest on Peruvian mountain peaks.
They don't hoard treasure. They collect antiques
Acquired from Arabs and shipped by Greeks.

There are sea-serpents in the boiling swell,
Great coiling snakes from the heart of Hell,
That can tell, by smell, where to start an oil well.
They're employed by BP, Gulf and Shell.

Our English dragons inhabit The Shires,
Where everyone admires these graceful flyers.
They start the stubble fires that the squire requires,
And are famed for their fairness as cricket umpires.

Then you've got your Welsh beast, muscly and red,
With skin-'n'-bone wings and a brutal head.
Ivor Evans kept one in his garden shed,
Though he now grows daffodils and leeks instead.

When I look at you,
Can you tell by my eyes
Whether that was true
Or a pack of lies?

Parasites

Far, far away in blue moonlight,
Flocks of dragons are taking flight.
Their scales are dull. Their eyes are bright.
Their vampire teeth stand sharp and white
Like stalactite and stalagmite.

On fields of dreams they'll graze tonight
To satisfy their appetite
For fantasy, far-fetched delight
And magic stories set alight
By wild adventures which excite.

Ours are the dreams on which they'll bite.
From worlds away, and far from sight,
They'll come as guests we don't invite
And read our minds like words we write
And feed on these while we sleep tight.

Our nightmares know this parasite.
With wisps of fear and twists of fright
We've something saying all's not right.
And we'd strike back with all our might
But, locked in sleep, we'll fight no fight.

Far, far away in blue moonlight,
Flocks of dragons are taking flight.
Their scales are dull. Their eyes are bright.
The pain we'll feel will be but slight
From sets of teeth so sharp and white.

The Magic of Dragons

She places aces on her tail,
Impales each with a fingernail,
And every ace becomes a six.
Dragon's doing magic tricks.

She's chucking coins into a pail
But slips each one beneath a scale.
No-one spots that it's a fix.
Dragon's doing magic tricks.

Her pyrotechnics never fail.
She breathes on things. They burn, but they'll
Return unburned in just two ticks.
Dragon's doing magic tricks.

She reads our minds like reading Braille.
She's right in every last detail.
Then coughs up candles with lit wicks.
Dragon's doing magic tricks.

Pigeons fly from under veils
Through clouds of smoke which she exhales,
Then ropes move up and down two sticks.
Dragon's doing magic tricks.

She introduces Abigail
And saws in half this poor female
But she's restored with two wand-flicks.
Dragon's doing magic tricks.

Wow! I'm amazed. "It's fake!" you wail.
How sad you are. Go home, tell-tale,
To walls and floors and life that's stale.
Real homes are more than planks and bricks.
Real lives need dragons, and their tricks.

All Night Long

And all night long our dragon sings
As preciously as diamond rings
Of flaming fragments plucked from strings
And only half-remembered things
And rumours raised on dreamy wings
Like water which the dowser brings
To thirsty lips from long-lost springs.

And all night long our dragon sings
How fate fantastically flings
Time's arrows and outrageous slings
At all our joys and sufferings
While melody's the sword it swings
At an acrobatic tune that clings
To power... just like queens and kings.

And all night long our dragon sings
For us and other underlings
And, through the day, small echoings
Return to strike like tiny stings
Which only cease when evenings
Each darken. Then the dragon sings...
And all night long it sings, it sings.

Rare Dragons

You'll seldom find a dragon with
No trace of the barbarian,
A sentimental gentle one
Who's not a slightly scary one.

There's surely not a dragon that
Is purely vegetarian,
That really cares for animals
And is a veterinarian.

Or one that looks at lots of books,
A qualified grammarian,
That has a love of literature
And works as a librarian.

No shaven-headed Buddhist nor
Your peaceful, hippy, hairy one,
Nor one who's into reggae who's
A dreadlocked Rastafarian.

The Disappearance of Chinese Dragons

Three thousand miles from the Philippine Isles
To the heights of Turkistan,
And all the way from Mandalay
To the coast of far Japan,

You'll find, depicted and displayed,
Dragons of every shape and shade,
Embroidered, painted, carved in jade
Or ivory, and jewel-inlaid.
Each treasured once, they're all now trade,
Their values set by prices paid.

From copper mines and camel lines
On dry Mongolia's barren plains
To Buddhist prayer and Yeti's lair
On high Tibetan mountain chains.

The dragon that they now parade's
A paper one which people made.
The actual creature's long decayed,
Its spirit cheapened and betrayed
With paste and paint that time will fade;
Its world of wonderment mislaid.

Three thousand miles from the Philippine Isles
To the heights of Turkistan,
And all the way from Mandalay
To the coast of far Japan,

No egg, no bone, no trace remains,
An empty throne where silence reigns,
A twilight zone, all loss, no gains.
This bird has flown. Its old moon wanes.
This crop's not grown, no fruits, no grains.
Its ghost is blown through these terrains.

Dragons don't Exist

Dragons, mate? They don't exist.
So cross them off your Christmas list.

We've no such things –
No snakes with wings.

Ask any archaeologist
If dragons do or don't exist.
He'll treat you like you're round the twist
So pardon me if I insist
That dragons simply don't exist.

We've no such things –
No snakes with wings,
No spikes, no scales,
No pointed tails.

If any college scientist
Suggested that they *might* exist
Then he or she would be dismissed.
Not me, cos I'm a realist.
I *know* that dragons don't exist.

We've no such things –
No snakes with wings,
No spikes, no scales,
No pointed tails,
No sudden death
By fiery breath,
No flying oral arsonist.

"Oh, such a creature *can't* exist,"
Says teacher and says naturalist.
It's pure Scotch mist, so let's desist
Cos dragons simply don't exist.

We've no such things –
No snakes with wings,
No spikes, no scales,
No pointed tails,
No sudden death
By fiery breath,
No rich rewards,
No treasure hoards.

The Blarney Stone must have been kissed
By those insisting they exist.
Oi! See this fist above my wrist?
It's yours right now if you persist,
Cos dragons *truly* don't exist!

He led us to
The dragon's lair,
Said, "I'll show you!"
And walked in there.

Then came a roar,
A scream, a moan,
And nothing more
Was ever known...

... or missed
Of the man who said dragons
Didn't exist.